THE DEMON BABYSITTER

Other books in the Nightmare Club series

THE
DEMON
BABYSITTER

BY

ANNIE GRAVES

ILLUSTRATED BY
GLENN McELHINNEY

Little Island

THE DEMON BABYSITTER 583 100 4

Published 2013
by Little Island
7 Kenilworth Park
Dublin 6W
Ireland

www.littleisland.ie

ISBN 978-1-908195-80-7

Book design by Fidelma Slattery @ Someday

Typeset in 'Trebuchet MS' (by Vincent Connare) and 'October Crow'
(by Chad Savage). Cover title typeface (also used in interior):
'Remnant' (by Chris Au), www.chrisau-design.co.uk

Printed in Poland by Drukarnia Skleniarz

Little Island receives financial assistance from
The Arts Council (An Chomhairle Ealaíon), Dublin, Ireland.

Supported by
The National Lottery®
through the Arts Council of Northern Ireland

10 9 8 7 6 5 4 3 2 1

To all survivors of evil babysitters

Annie Graves is twelve years old, and she has no intention of ever growing up. She is, conveniently, an orphan, and lives at an undisclosed address in the Glasnevin area of Dublin with her pet toad, Much Misunderstood, and a small black kitten, Hugh Shalby Nameless.

You needn't think she goes to school — pah! — or has anything as dull as brothers and sisters or hobbies, but let's just say she keeps a large black cauldron on the stove.

This is not her first book. She has written seven, so far, none of which is her first.

Publisher's note: we did try to take a picture of Annie, but her face just kept fading away. We have sent our camera for investigation, but suspect the worst.

THANK YOU!!

I don't know what's with this acknowledgement thing that my publishers keep banging on about. It's not like I had any *help* with this story or anything. OK, OK, so maybe Alice Stevens did mutter something to me one day at a bus stop about how she knew this girl who'd had this babysitter who ...

But that was ALL. Cross my heart and hope to live.

(HAPPY NOW?)

Listen, kids, this is kinda scary because, let's face it, we all get babysat sometimes (except me of course, I don't do grown-ups), so the thought of a demon babysitter is a little ... shall we say, unsettling.

But I didn't make up the story. It was Becky, and she's such a nice girl. Always tells the truth.

Mostly tells the truth anyway.

'Have you ever had a really awful babysitter?' Becky asked when the lights were turned off and we only had Joshua's flickering torch to see by. 'One who bossed and bullied you?'

Nobody answered her.

Nobody said a word.

'Well, I have,' Becky went on in her nice-girl voice. Funny how scary a nice-girl voice can be sometimes. 'Her name was Dervla.'

'Doesn't sound like a scary story to me,' I said.

Becky just blinked at me.

'Except "Dervla" sounds a bit ... devilish, don't you think?' she said after a moment. 'Would you like to hear about her?'

We all swallowed silently and nodded in the torchlight.

And this is the story Becky told ...

Dervla was my next-door neighbour.

She had frizzy red hair, which she tied back with a yellow ribbon.

She also had big freckles and squinty eyes.

None of the kids on our road liked her.

She was always telling us what to do and what not to do.

Her voice was high and squeaky: 'Don't do this, don't do that, I'm telling …'

And she did.

You didn't get away with anything if Dervla was around.

The day Dervla turned fourteen was a dark day for the kids in our estate.

Now she was old enough to babysit.

Of course all the parents *loved* Dervla because she was so 'responsible', so 'grown-up'.

When Dervla babysat, she sent kids to bed when it was still light outside.

We were never allowed to watch TV and had to eat whatever she put in front of us.

If we didn't do what Dervla told us, she went straight to our parents.

She *lied* to them.

She told Karl's parents he tried to set fire to his mother's favourite dress.

She said Susie was swinging from one of the ceiling lights.

According to Dervla, Brenda was a witch who brewed potions with her mother's perfumes.

She was a fantastic liar, and she'd say *anything* to make sure kids did what they were told. And they did.

They ate broccoli and cauliflower and carrots.

They brushed their teeth — *twice*.

They even did all their homework.

(Dervla gave *extra* homework if they finished their real homework too quickly.)

They cleaned their rooms and bathrooms.

They acted like Dervla's slaves.

EXCEPT ME.

I wasn't going to stand for this.

I was going to rebel.

So whenever Dervla told me to do something, I did the exact opposite.

If she told me to go to bed, I ran outside to play. Even *after* it was dark.

If she told me to eat my vegetables, I stuffed my face with sweets and chocolate milk.

If she told me to do my homework, I scribbled all over it.

The other kids loved me.

I was their hero.

I did what everyone else was too afraid
to do.

But Dervla was a pretty serious enemy.

She started telling the most terrible lies about me.

At first, they were just the usual things:

I wrote on the wall.

I put spiders in her hair.

I made prank phone calls to China.

Then it got worse.

She said she'd caught me driving the car.

I was supposed to have shot birds with a homemade slingshot.

She even said that I buried my dog alive. (Seymour showed up safe and sound the next day.)

I got in more and more trouble
with my parents.

I was grounded for months.

They took my computer games away.

I got a piece of coal for my birthday.

BUT I DID NOT GIVE UP.

I cut off Dervla's favourite doll's head and threw one of her books in the fire.

I spat in her tea and I really did put spiders in her hair.

Pretty soon she didn't even have to lie about what I'd done.

At first I just didn't like Dervla because she was a bossy babysitter.

But after a while it was more than that.

I began to get a weird feeling about her.

It started when I noticed this strange smell when she was around. Kind of a strong smell of burning. Like barbecued meat.

I also noticed her itching.

She was always scratching her head under the yellow ribbon.

But then something really weird happened.

It made me think something *very* creepy was going on.

I was in the kitchen, hatching my latest plan against Dervla.

I'd decided to pop some popcorn and maybe forget to put the lid on the saucepan.

I turned on the cooker.

Just as I was getting out the popcorn, I heard Dervla growling, 'What on earth are you doing?'

'Nothing, Dervla,' I said in my sweetest voice.

But she wasn't buying it. She never did. She knew me too well.

'Don't lie to me,' she snarled. 'I'm keeping my eye on you, you little wretch.'

She was whispering, but her voice wasn't soft. It was hard and angry.

And then she put her hand on the hot stove.

I almost screamed aloud.

But she looked straight at me and said, 'What?'

She didn't even flinch.

SHE

DIDN'T

FEEL A

THING!!!!

18

From then on, I started to be a little afraid of Dervla.

I watched her when she wasn't looking, and I noticed weird stuff.

Her skin looked strange in certain lights. Almost red. And her freckles seemed to have faded.

Sometimes when she spoke, her voice didn't sound like a girl's at all. It was deep and sounded like some horrible growl.

Then she'd clear her throat and her voice would be back to normal.

One horrifying night, I saw Dervla eat a spider that was crawling along the counter.

She popped it in her mouth.

JUST LIKE THAT.

From then on, I knew that Dervla was different.

EVIL.

Not evil
in a teenage
girl way, BUT REALLY EVIL.

One night when she was babysitting me, we had this big fight.

Dervla grabbed the TV remote as soon as she arrived.

When I started yelling, she dragged me upstairs and locked me in my bedroom.

I heard her laughing maniacally as she turned the key in the lock and went downstairs.

Of course this was not a problem for me.

When you're in a war with a devil like Dervla, you have to have a few tricks up your sleeve.

I had these really powerful stink bombs.

They were small and made of glass with some kind of yellow vomit-coloured liquid inside.

I shinned down the drainpipe and came in the back door.

I crept into the TV room where she was sitting.

I had the stink bombs in my pocket.

She was on the couch, facing away from me.

I tiptoed up behind her, holding my breath so I wouldn't laugh.

Just as I was reaching for the stink bombs, I noticed something that made me stop.

Poking out of Dervla's frizzy red hair were

I looked at her hand lying on the armrest.

There was something very wrong with it.

Instead of a freckly pale hand with slightly chewed nails, there was a reddish hand with long fingers and thick black nails.

Then, with a terrible slow slither, a thin forked tail emerged from behind the couch.

I got that awful sick feeling in my stomach.

I covered my mouth so I wouldn't scream. And I slowly backed out of the room.

The floor creaked.

As soon as I heard that creak, it felt like everything froze for a second.

And then, slowly, Dervla's head started to turn around.

It was definitely her.

I had kind of been hoping it was an imposter.

But no, it was my babysitter all right.

My demon babysitter.

Except that now her eyes were completely black and she was smiling at me through pointed teeth.

'Well, Becky. Misbehaving again, are we? This time I'm not going to tell your parents. I'll deal with you myself.'

She said these last words with a growl and made a jump at me.

I threw a chair in front of the demon and ran out of the room.

I heard an angry howl as she tripped over the chair.

I ran up the stairs, two steps at a time, burst into my parents' room and crawled into my best hiding place.

It was an air vent that I can fit in. I've hidden there before. I was sure I would be safe there.

After a while, I heard these horrible footsteps.

They were heavy but also had a clicking sound, as if claws were scratching the wooden floor.

The door opened slowly.

The creature began walking around the room, her claws clicking, her tail swishing back and forth.

As Dervla walked past the air vent, the air was filled with a horrible stench.

The smell of burning meat.

I held my breath.

Finally Dervla turned to leave.

I was sure she hadn't seen me.

But just as she put her hand on the door handle, she began to sniff the air.

Turning around, the demon looked right at the air vent.

In three steps she ran across the room and ripped open the air vent with a snarl.

She grabbed me by my hood and lifted me off the floor.

I smashed one of my stink bombs onto the demon's head.

Dervla roared and coughed and spluttered.

I hit her with a lamp. The demon went down. I had knocked her out.

Then I got my dad's bicycle lock and locked her in an old abandoned shed down by the river.

I feed her every day.

At first all the kids on the road were delighted.

They chanted, 'The wicked witch is dead,' and threw a doll that looked like Dervla in the river.

But when Dervla didn't turn up, everyone started to feel sorry for her.

They started to look for her.

They stuck up posters.

MISSING

Sweet girl called Dervla

People complained that I had been too mean to her.

Everyone forgot how nasty she had always been to us.

They said she was just trying to look out for us.

I got sick and tired of everyone feeling sorry for her, so I told the other kids what really happened.

Now I'm more popular than ever.

Some kids even call me the demon hunter.

The little kids follow me everywhere, begging me to tell them about the demon babysitter.

So I do.

(I mean, who doesn't enjoy a little attention?)

I explain the best way to spot a demon and what to feed them. (Charred spiders, in case you're wondering.)

They think I'm an expert on the subject.

To be fair, I *am* a bit of an expert on the subject.

Who else do *you* know who's faced a demon and lived to tell the story?

That's what I thought.

And it's not just devils that I know about.

I could tell you about witches and ogres and goblins and gremlins.

If you keep your eyes and ears open, it's amazing what you can spot.

Or maybe I just have the knack for it.

For instance, I'm pretty certain that my new babysitter's a vampire.

All the kids on the road like her.

They say she's much nicer than Dervla because she lets them stay up late and watch cartoons, but I saw through that straight away.

I KNOW the signs.

Doesn't eat garlic.

Pale skin.

Pointy teeth.

Sure, she goes out during the day, but everyone knows real vampires can go out any time they like. That's what makes them so dangerous.

So I guess Dervla will be getting some company soon.

I mean, *someone* has to do *something*.

And I'm more than happy to help.